Nate the Great
and the
SNOWY TRAIL

Marjorie Weinman Sharmat
illustrated by Marc Simont

READ ALL THESE

Nate the Great
DETECTIVE STORIES

BY MARJORIE WEINMAN SHARMAT
WITH ILLUSTRATIONS BY MARC SIMONT

Dell

ISBN 0-440-46276-2

US $4.50 / $6.99 CAN

Nate the Great
and the
SNOWY TRAIL

Nate the Great
and the
SNOWY TRAIL

by
Marjorie Weinman Sharmat
illustrated by Marc Simont

A Yearling Book

Published by
Bantam Doubleday Dell Books for Young Readers
a division of
Random House, Inc.
1540 Broadway
New York, New York 10036

ISBN: 0-440-46276-2

Reprinted by arrangement with The Putnam Publishing Group Inc.

Printed in the United States of America

January 1984

40 39 38 37

CWO

I, Nate the Great,

am a detective.

This morning I was a cold detective.

I was standing in the snow

with my dog, Sludge,

building a snow dog

and a snow detective.

They looked like Sludge and me.

They were cold and white and wet.

And so were we.

Rosamond came along.

Rosamond is strange most of the time.

Today was one of those times.

She was pulling her four cats,

Super Hex, Big Hex, Little Hex,

and Plain Hex, on a sled.

She went up to the snow detective.

"I lost your birthday present,"

she said to him.

The snow detective did not answer.

I did.

"That detective is one hour old.

Why are you giving him

a birthday present?"

Rosamond looked at me.

"Oh, it's for *you*," she said.

"My birthday is July 12," I said.

"This is the middle of winter."

"I believe in giving early,"

Rosamond said.

She pointed to her sled.

9

"I was pulling your present
and my cats
on my sled,
but the present fell off
along the way."

10

"Do you know when and where
it happened?" I asked.
"Yes," Rosamond said.
"I was feeling drippy.
Snow from the trees
was falling on me.

11

Then all of a sudden
the sled felt lighter.
I turned around
and looked at it.
Your present was gone.
I walked around and around
in the snow,
but I couldn't find it.
It has a Happy Birthday card on it.
Will you look for your present?"
I, Nate the Great,
knew that Rosamond's present
must be strange.
But I am a detective.
And the present was lost.
"I, Nate the Great,

will take your case,"

I said.

"Tell me what the present is,

so I will know

what to look for."

"Oh, I can't tell you *that*,"
Rosamond said.
"It would spoil the surprise.
But it could be
big or small
or medium size
or square or pointy
or flat or bulgy.
Or red or blue
or green or black
or plaid or polka-dotted or . . ."
Suddenly I, Nate the Great,
knew something.
I did not want this case.
"How can I find something
if I do not know

what I am looking for?" I asked.

"You're a great detective,

aren't you?" Rosamond said.

She walked away

and pulled her cats behind her.

Sludge and I went inside.

I left a note for my mother.

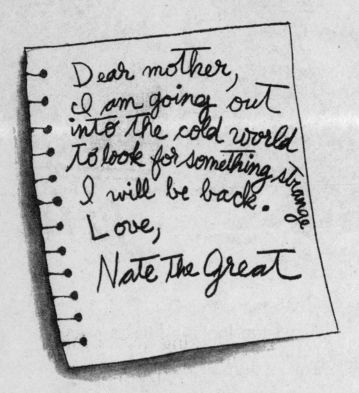

Dear mother,
I am going out
into the cold world
to look for something strange
I will be back.
Love,
Nate The Great

I put on a dry pair of mittens.

Then Sludge and I

went out into the snow.

Rosamond had given me a clue,

but she did not know it.

She had told me

that the sled felt lighter

the moment the present was not on it.

I, Nate the Great, knew

that the present must be heavy.

But it had to fit on the sled

with the four cats.

So I knew it was not as big

as a dead tree

or a broken sofa

or an old door

or some other strange thing

that only Rosamond could think of.

I, Nate the Great,
was glad about that.
I looked down at the snow.
I saw Rosamond's footprints.
I saw sled marks.
Some came toward my house.
Some went away from my house.

Hmm. I, Nate the Great,
had an idea.
If I followed the prints
that led toward my house,
I could see the path
that Rosamond took to my house.

Perhaps the present

was lying in the snow

along the path.

Sludge and I

walked forward in the snow

while we watched Rosamond's footprints

going backward in the snow.

It was a long, cold walk.

The snow crunched.

Icicles hung from the trees.

All at once,

under a tree,

Rosamond's footprints

went in a wide circle.

Around and around.

This must be
where she lost my present
and was looking for it!
Sludge sniffed the snow.

I looked in the snow

for a package

or the snow print

of a package.

But the snow

next to the sled marks

was unbroken.

I, Nate the Great, was puzzled.

How could something

drop off the sled

and not be in the snow

or leave a mark

in the snow?

There were no footprints either.

So I, Nate the Great, knew

that no one had come along

and taken the birthday present.
But how did the present
get off the sled,
and where was it?
"This is a tough, ice-cold case,"
I said to Sludge.
Sludge shivered.

We trudged on.

We saw Annie and her dog, Fang.

Sludge shivered some more.

He was afraid of Fang.

I, Nate the Great,

was afraid of Fang.

Fang ran toward us.

Sludge leaped over

a big pile of snow.

I had never seen Sludge

leap that high.

"Fang is so friendly,"

Annie said.

She was making a snow dog.

It looked just like Fang.

It had icicles for teeth.

They were long and sharp and pointed.

Just like Fang's teeth.

But I liked them better.

They would melt.

I said, "I am looking

for a heavy birthday present

that could be

big or small

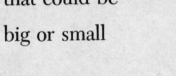

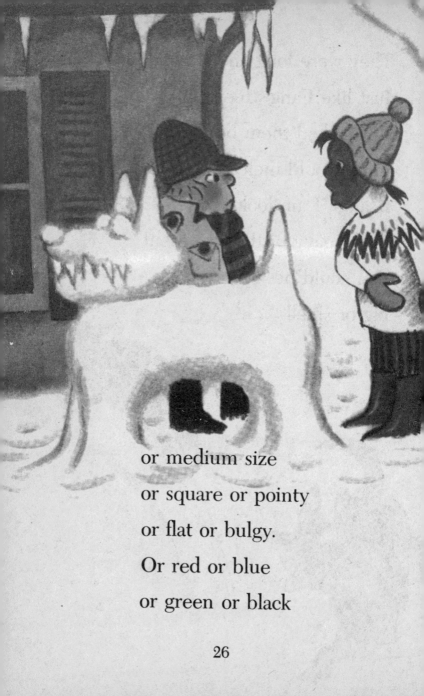

or medium size

or square or pointy

or flat or bulgy.

Or red or blue

or green or black

26

or plaid or polka-dotted

or any number of things.

But there is one thing for sure.

It is strange."

"Rosamond was here," Annie said.

"But she left.

I have not seen anything strange

since then."

"What did she do and say?"

I asked.

"Well," Annie said, "I was inside

drinking hot chocolate.

Rosamond came in.

She told me she had

a birthday present for you.

She said it was outside

on her sled

with her four cats.

She wouldn't tell me

what it was.

But she said it was

the most beautiful present ever."

"That is a good clue," I said.

"Rosamond thinks scorpions and spiders

and bats are beautiful.

So I, Nate the Great,

now know I am looking

for something ugly."

I thanked Annie for her help.

I called to Sludge.
He was hiding behind
a pile of snow.
We started out again.
"We are looking for something
strange, heavy, and ugly,"
I said.
I saw a snow castle up ahead.
Claude was sitting inside it.
Claude was always losing things.

"Look what I found," Claude said.

"A snow castle."

"Your luck is changing," I said.

"Perhaps you have found

a strange, heavy, and ugly

birthday present?"

"Who would want to find *that*?"

Claude asked.

It was a good question.

But I, Nate the Great,
did not want to answer it.
"I saw an ugly birthday card
at a store this morning,"
Claude said. "Rosamond was buying it."
"Aha!" I said.
"What else did Rosamond buy?"
"She bought six cartons
of milk," Claude said.
I, Nate the Great,
was sorry to hear that.
"Six cartons of milk?" I said.
I, Nate the Great, did not want
a birthday present
that was cold and white and wet.
I was already colder

and whiter

and wetter

than I had ever been.

I said good-by to Claude.

"Enjoy your castle," I said.

"Don't lose it."

"How can I lose a castle?"

Claude asked.

"Only you know how," I said.

Sludge and I went to Rosamond's house.

I said, "I do not know
where my birthday present is,
but I know *what* it is.
Please open your refrigerator."
Rosamond opened her refrigerator.
I saw tuna fish, cat food,
and a melting snow cat inside.
"Aha!" I said. "No milk!
You bought six cartons of milk
this morning, but now you have none.
You put them on your sled
to take to me.
And that was the birthday present
you lost on the way to my house."
Rosamond took out the snow cat
and licked it.

"Why would I buy you
a strange present
like six cartons of milk?"
she asked.

I, Nate the Great,

knew better

than to tell Rosamond why.

"The milk was for my cats,"

Rosamond said. "They drank it up."

I, Nate the Great,

was getting nowhere.

This case was more ice-cold than ever.

I tried to think warm thoughts.

I thought about my warm house.

I thought about warm pancakes.

I said good-by to Rosamond.

Sludge and I trudged home

through the snow.

Sludge was still shivering.

At home I ate some warm pancakes.

I gave Sludge a warm bone.

Sludge is a great detective.

But all he had done

was shiver and leap

in the snow.

Leap in the snow.

Leap. Hmm.

I, Nate the Great,

thought about that.

Did Sludge know something
I didn't know?
I thought about footprints
and sled marks
in the snow
and snow that had no marks in it,

and six cartons of milk
and other chilly things.
The milk
was for Rosamond's four cats.
But she bought *six* cartons.
Who or what needed
the two extra cartons of milk?
And what would Rosamond think
was the most beautiful
present ever?

Suddenly I, Nate the Great,

knew what my present was,

and where it was,

and how it got there.

I said to Sludge,

"I know what is heavy, strange, and ugly

and can get off a sled

without landing in the snow.

The case is solved,

and you were a big help.

But we must go out

into the cold world again."

Sludge and I went back

to the place

where Rosamond had lost the present.

This time I did not look down
at the snow.
I looked up
at the tree.
There was my birthday present
sitting high up in the tree!

It was heavy and strange
and ugly, all right.
It was the biggest cat
I had ever seen.
It was bigger than Super Hex.
It was almost as big as Sludge.
It was almost as big as me,
Nate the Great.
It was a monster.
It had a Happy Birthday card
hanging from a ribbon
around its neck.
Now I knew why Rosamond
had bought six cartons of milk
when she had only four cats.
This monster cat

she was giving me

was so big

it needed two cartons of milk.

And I knew why

I had not seen the birthday present

or marks from the birthday present

in the snow

next to the sled.

The birthday present

had not touched the snow.

It had *leaped*

from the sled

into the tree.

Now I knew everything

except what I was going to do

with my birthday present.

Sludge and I went back
to Rosamond's house.
"The case is solved," I said.
"I found my birthday present
up a tree."
"Oh, good!" Rosamond said.

"His name is Super Duper Hex.

I got him from the same place

I got Super Hex, Big Hex,

Little Hex, and Plain Hex.

I wanted to keep him.

But he fights with my cats and wins.

He scratches, claws, and bites.

But nobody's perfect.

Happy birthday!"

Sometimes, being a great detective

is not great.

Sludge and I trudged home

through the snow.

We passed the tree

where my birthday present

was still sitting.

He liked it there.

Maybe he would sit there

forever.

Or maybe he would jump down

and follow us home.

Sludge and I kept walking.

I, Nate the Great,
knew two new things.
Never look up.
And never look back.
Sludge and I went home
and sat by the fire.
I was glad I had
only one birthday a year.

Marjorie Weinman Sharmat has written more than 130 books for children and young adults, which have been translated into seventeen languages. She lives with her husband, author Mitchell Sharmat, in Tucson, Arizona. They have two sons, Craig and Andrew.

Look for Marjorie Weinman Sharmat's other Random House Children's Books series, Duz Shedd.

Marc Simont won the Caldecott Medal for his artwork in *A Tree Is Nice* by Janice May Udry. He has illustrated twenty books in the Nate the Great series. He lives in West Cornwall, Connecticut.

Nate the Great
and the
SNOWY TRAIL

by
Marjorie Weinman Sharmat
illustrated by Marc Simont

Nate the Great, super sleuth, has his work cut out for him when Rosamond loses his birthday present. He and his faithful dog, Sludge, must face snow, ice, and ferocious-looking Fang, Annie's dog, to solve the case. But how can Nate find his missing present when Rosamond won't tell him what it is?

"Brisk and bright as always, with pictures of a lovably scowling Nate and a voguishly strange Rosamond . . . for added appeal." —*Kirkus Reviews*

"Simont's exuberant drawings . . . illustrate Sharmat's new . . . book . . . Readers will have a dandy time following the case and will sympathize with Nate's wish that he had failed to solve it when he finds the dismaying 'present.'"
—*Publishers Weekly*

"The tongue-in-cheek mystery unfolds briskly. Simont's . . . cartoons are in tune with Sharmat's comic touch." —*Booklist*

US $4.50 / $6.99 CAN

ISBN 0-440-46276-2

46276

0 71009 00450 4

A Yearling Book
New York
RL: 2.1
006-009